COLETTE CADDLE

THE CRIMINAL'S WIFE

Colette Caddle lives in Dublin with her husband and two sons. She is the author of fifteen novels including *From This Moment On, First We Take Manhattan and Red Letter Day*. Her books are available in paperback, audio, large print and ebook format and have been translated into several languages. For more information, check out colettecaddle.com. Like Colette Caddle Books on Facebook or follow her on Twitter.

NEW ISLAND

THE CRIMINAL'S WIFE
First published 2015
by New Island
16 Priory Office Park
Stillorgan
Co Dublin

www.newisland.ie

PRINT ISBN: 978-1-84840-411-3

British Library Cataloguing Data. A CIP catalogue record
for this book is available from the British Library

Typeset by JVR Creative India
Cover design by New Island Books
Printed by SPRINT-print Ltd.

New Island received financial assistance from
The Arts Council (*An Comhairle Ealaíon*), Dublin, Ireland

10 9 8 7 6 5 4 3 2 1

Dear Reader,

On behalf of myself and the other contributing authors, I would like to welcome you to the eighth Open Door series. The books in this series are written and designed to introduce new and emergent readers to the writings of many bestselling authors who have sold millions of books worldwide. We hope that you enjoy the books and that reading becomes a lasting pleasure in your life.

Warmest wishes,

Patricia Scanlan.

Patricia Scanlan
Series Editor

Please visit www.newisland.ie for information on all eight Open Door series.

Chapter One

'Gerry O'Dowd has been taken out.'

As his superintendent swept into the room, Tom Doyle looked up from the small mountain of files he had been half-heartedly reading. The boss stood in front of his desk. His hands were behind his back, his chest puffed out. He nodded his bald head, clearly relishing the moment. Shay Scanlan was hot on his heels. He closed the door and leaned against it, his eyes gleaming with excitement.

Tom settled back in his chair and waited, grateful for the interruption. He had been in Dublin for a couple of months now and spent the entire time either slogging through old case files or attending meetings that dragged on and on. He wasn't good cooped up in an office. It did his head in. Even spending hours staking out suspects in a hot, cramped car with a partner who burped and farted was better than office work.

'Always good to know there is one less drug baron in the world,' Tom said. 'How did it happen?'

'He was coming out of the post office after collecting his dole money when two guys on a bike pulled up. They put a couple of bullets in his head and another few in his chest,' Shay told him.

'They weren't taking any chances,' Tom observed.

'No.' Superintendent Denis Flynn crossed to the window to look down on the busy street below. 'All very cold and well planned except they picked too busy a location and we've got a witness. I'm putting you on the case, Doyle. But I don't want you doing a Rambo. This is a team effort and I want to be kept fully up to date.'

Tom sat up. He was finally getting some action? He felt the adrenalin start to pump as it hadn't in a bloody long time. He had begun to think it never would again. But his excitement was quickly replaced by misgivings. Sure, he was a good detective. He'd been doing the job eight years now and had earned his stripes, but he was still the new boy in Dublin. 'What? Why me?'

Flynn didn't turn around. 'You don't want it?'

'Of course I do,' Tom said immediately. 'Just curious.'

'The suspect is someone you know a lot better than we do.'

3

Tom froze. Only one name came to mind but he had never got mixed up in the Dublin scene, or if he had, it had totally passed them by. He swallowed the bile at the back of his throat. 'Mossie Maher?'

Flynn spun round and smiled. 'Bingo.'

'Are you sure?' Tom knew Maher was capable of taking on the Dublin low-life, but he had a good thing going in the south-west of the country, why would he bother? Flynn glared and Tom backtracked when Shay shot him a warning glance. He had a knack for pissing off his superiors, but even he realised that doing it this early in a new job wasn't a good plan. 'Sorry, it's just that I never thought he'd be interested in branching out at his time of life.'

'Power and greed are great motivators and who knows what goes on in a mind as warped as Maher's,' Flynn said.

4

'True,' Tom said, wishing O'Dowd had taken out Maher and not the other way around.

'The point is we finally have a chance to nail the bastard,' Flynn said. 'Your team in Limerick will be delighted.'

Tom stood up. 'I better get over to the crime scene.'

'No, Davis and Nolan are already there. Right now I think you and Inspector Scanlan should go and have a word with Mrs O'Dowd and we'll have a meeting here at eight.'

What the hell? Tom looked at Scanlan, who gave a shrug. This was nuts. The woman wouldn't want to see the razzers on her doorstep hours after her husband had been killed. Even if she knew anything, she wouldn't tell them. That type never did. They didn't look to the Gardaí for justice. They dealt with it themselves. The house would probably be full of low-life scum tanked up on booze and drugs. Walking in there was just looking for trouble. What was Flynn's game? 'Would it not be better to leave it until after the funeral, Super?' Tom asked.

'Not at all. We have to comfort and support the grieving widow,' Flynn grinned. 'Don't worry, Doyle. You might know the Limerick players but I know the score in Dublin. We need to move quickly.'

Yes, they needed to move quickly. They needed to be at the scene. They needed to talk to witnesses, to check out the CCTV, they needed to arrest Mossie Maher and search his house. Talking to the widow was a waste of time. But he supposed he'd better go along with it to keep Flynn sweet. 'Of course I've heard of O'Dowd and his family but I don't know all of his history. Anything in particular you want us to find out?'

'Shay can fill you in about them on the way and I'll let you decide what questions need asking. Come on, lads, shift yourselves.' The superintendent headed for the door and Scanlan opened it for him.

'What is this, some kind of test for the new boy?' Tom asked when they were alone.

Scanlan grinned. 'No, I'd say he just wants you to get to know the O'Dowds. We've been dealing with their crap for so long, it's hard to be neutral anymore. Also they hate us. They might respond better to a new face.'

Tom strapped on his gun and grabbed his leather jacket. 'Then let's go.'

He slid the passenger seat back as far as it would go to suit his long legs and held on to the handle above his head as Shay swung the silver Avensis out of the car

7

park. He turned it in the direction of the sprawling estate on the outskirts of Swords. As he drove, Shay gave him a potted history of one of Dublin's most powerful criminal families.

'The father was a small-time crook, handling stolen goods, money laundering, that sort of thing. He died in Mountjoy jail of a heart attack about five years ago. Gerry always had much bigger ideas. He started the whole drugs operation He was pretty much running things in North County Dublin and Louth. A real thug! Robbie is next on the list. He's a cold, cruel bastard. He's been arrested on drugs and firearm charges more times than you've had hot dinners. He's in The Joy at the moment for GBH. He beats the wife up too.'

'Is he an addict?'

'Ah, yes and so is she. Your heart would go out to the kids. They will most likely be druggies themselves, and dealing by the time they're twelve.'

'Save your pity for the kids they will be selling to,' Tom retorted.

'We don't get to choose the family we're born into,' Scanlan pointed out.

'Whatever. What about the youngest brother?'

'Jude. He's only twenty-six but I think he might step into Gerry's shoes. He's smart and hard. He doesn't drink or do drugs. He has never been inside. We know for a fact that he is a big part of the family business.'

'How come he's managed to avoid prison?' Tom asked.

'He's the next generation. He does business online and leaves others to do the dirty work. He imports the drugs and, word is, sells some that way too.'

'But there must be a trail,' Tom insisted. 'Have you got search warrants and taken his laptop?'

Shay looked at him in disgust. 'Of course we have but we found nothing. We think he works through smart phones. A couple of times when we've picked him up we found smashed ones and forensics couldn't get any information out of them.'

'We need a good hacker on the team.'

Shay grinned. 'We've got one. He's a university student.'

'Yes, but he hasn't found anything. Tell him to keep studying.' Tom wondered yet again why Mossie Maher would take on these Dublin hoods.

Chapter Two

Scanlan pulled into the estate and Tom looked around at the rows of charmless, terraced three-storey houses. 'This is where Gerry O'Dowd lived?' He was amazed.

'It's just one of his properties. He has an apartment in the city centre and a mansion on a couple of acres in County Meath.'

'And he was on the dole?' Tom said.

Scanlan chuckled. 'Of course. The apartment is in the mother's name. The Meath place belongs to a friend who spends all of his time in Spain. They just house sit.'

'Of course they do,' Tom scoffed.

Shay turned right and pulled up outside the first house on the left. It looked like all the others. It also seemed deserted. 'Looks like no one is home. Still, we're here now, we may as well ring the doorbell.'

'You haven't told me anything about the wife,' Tom said as they got out of the car.

Scanlan smirked. 'Rose? Let's just say she's one of a kind.'

Tom could imagine. He'd met many gangsters' wives through the years. They usually fell into one of three kinds. Battered women who were terrified to open their mouths. Drug addicts who made no sense when they did speak, or hard-faced bitches who cursed loudly on seeing a guard on the doorstep.

He rang the doorbell but there was no answer. Scanlan went to the front window and pressed his face to the glass, then turned to him and shook his head. Tom was just heading back to the car when he heard a baby crying. He stopped and met the Scanlan's eyes.

'They have a kid,' Shay confirmed.

Tom retraced his steps and held his finger on the bell for a few seconds. He rapped the door knocker for good measure. Moments later he saw a shadow in the hall. The door was flung open by a woman holding a toddler who stared at them from round, curious eyes. He let out an enormous fart and started to smile, revealing six tiny white teeth. 'Poo!' he said, looking directly at Tom.

'Poo!' agreed Tom, holding his nose and pretending to faint. The little boy clapped his hands in delight, giving a belly laugh.

'What do you want?'

Tom was surprised by the sharp, cultured tone and for the first time looked past the child at the mother. She glared at him from startling green eyes that flashed angrily. She had perfect creamy skin. Her lips were full and she had a neat but curvy figure. A mane of dark, silky hair hung halfway down her back. She was nothing short of stunning and he couldn't take his eyes off her.

When he said nothing, Scanlan stepped forward to fill the silence. 'Sorry to intrude at a time like this, Mrs O'Dowd, I'm Inspector Scanlan—'

'I know who you are,' she snapped.

'And this is Detective Inspector Doyle.'

Her eyes returned to Tom and he felt her studying him. 'Sorry for your loss, Mrs O'Dowd,' he murmured.

She held his gaze, checking to see if he was genuine and then gave a short nod. 'Thank you.'

'We won't take up much of your time. We just want a quick chat.' He smiled at the little boy.

'I can't talk now. It's my son's bath time.' She went to shut the door on them but Tom had stepped closer. The toddler reached out to him.

'How old is this fine little man?' he asked and grinned when the child grabbed at his finger and hung on to it with a surprisingly strong grip.

'Fourteen months,' she said softly.

Tom's heart clenched. His child would have been about the same age if . . .

'Up!' The child held his arms out to him.

Rose looked in surprise at her son and held him closer. 'No, Toby.'

He frowned at her. 'Up!'

As the child struggled in her arms, she relented and allowed Tom to take him and stood back to let them in.

Scanlan looked at him, eyebrows raised. 'Interesting tactic,' he murmured as she led them into a small but comfortable living room.

A toy plastic train sat in the middle of the floor and the baby beamed at Tom and pointed. 'Choo-choo.'

'That's a great choo-choo.' Tom sat down on the rug with the child. He began to run the train around the little boy, with sound effects, making him laugh again. Rose O'Dowd stood looking down at them. She smiled when her son looked up at her in delight. Tom stared, mesmerised at the transformation. His eyes travelled from the pretty dimples, down the long white throat, to the modest neckline of her simple black cotton T-shirt. Her floral skirt that was tight on her hips flared out in layers to her feet. Even her feet were pretty in simple white terry flip-flops. How the hell did a bastard like Gerry O'Dowd snare a beautiful woman like Rose? His eyes were drawn back to the full, pink lips. She had been well named.

'Now, Mrs O'Dowd, can you tell us a little bit about this morning?' Scanlan started.

'No,' she snapped. 'Not in front of Toby.'

He stared at her in disbelief and then looked at his boss for guidance. His phone beeped and he took it out and glanced at it. 'I need to take this, sir.'

'Go ahead. I'll hang on here while Toby has his bath.'

'Yes, sir.' Scanlan stood up and left them, shaking his head slightly.

'Thank you,' she said when they heard the front door close.

He smiled up at her. 'No problem.'

'Bath time, Toby.' She bent to lift her son but immediately his arms were around Tom's neck.

'Bath! Up!'

She looked embarrassed. 'I'm sorry, he seems to have taken quite a shine to you.'

'No problem.' Tom laughed and swung the child on to his shoulders, making him squeal with delight. 'Let's go!'

Tom stood at the end of the bath and blew bubbles for the little boy, diverting him as Rose knelt and shampooed his dark curls. The position gave Tom a distracting view of her cleavage. When she went to lift him out Toby kicked his feet in delight, sending water everywhere.

'Oh, no, you're soaked,' Rose said, looking in horror at his shirt.

'So are you,' he said, his eyes drawn to her wet T-shirt. He looked up and realised that she was watching him watching her. Feeling like a guilty schoolboy, he turned away and gave all of his attention to Toby. He kept it there until the child was tucked up in the cot and his dark lashes started to flutter.

She smiled, stroking Toby's cheek. 'I think he's gone.'

'He's a great kid,' Tom whispered.

'Yes, he is.'

Rose switched on the monitor, turned off the light and they went downstairs. Tom knew he should call Scanlan back in but he wanted to spend some time alone with this woman. He knew that there was a much better chance of her opening up without Scanlan in the room. She sat down in the armchair, tucked her legs underneath her and rested her chin on her hand. Her hair fell like a curtain over one shoulder. 'How can I help you?'

Concentrate, Doyle, he told himself and fumbled for his notebook, feeling like a fool under her patient gaze. 'Okay, Mrs O'Dowd—'

'Call me Rose.'

He nodded. 'And I'm Tom. Sorry, I know you could probably do without this but I just want to ask you a few questions.'

She smiled. 'Usually when the Guards come round here they don't waste time talking.' She waved a hand at the bare mantelpiece. 'I stopped replacing the ornaments long ago.'

'Sorry,' he mumbled.

'No need to apologise. Gerry wasn't exactly an altar boy.'

He shook his head and sighed. 'You are a remarkable woman. So calm, and yet this must be the worst day of your life.'

She smiled the most beautiful smile. 'No, Detective Inspector, not at all. Today my life begins.'

Chapter Three

He thought about her words all the way back to the station. Scanlan had come in before he could ask what she meant, and for some reason Tom did not want to mention it in front of him. Instead he sat back and let Shay ask the questions. When they were leaving she had given him a grateful smile for letting her off the hook. And why had he? Because of her beauty? Because her little son had tugged on his heartstrings?

'You managed to thaw the snow queen,' Scanlan said. 'That's the most civil statement she's ever given.'

'Perhaps that's because she no longer has to worry about what her husband will say.'

'Good point, not that we learned anything.'

Tom did not agree. Rose might not have been able to shed any light on who might have killed her husband, but she had given him a glimpse of her feelings. He was pretty sure that she had not loved Gerry O'Dowd. She seemed relieved or maybe even happy that he was dead.

'Still, you got to meet our Rose. A stunner, isn't she? Great arse. I wouldn't say no to a bit of that posh totty.'

Tom frowned. He didn't like Shay talking about her like that. 'The woman has class. She's not involved in the business, is she?' God, he hoped not. She had seemed so lovely, intelligent and so gentle with Toby.

'As far as we know she isn't, but her brother was a small-time dealer for a time.'

Tom's ears pricked up. 'Was?'

'He got out of the game and emigrated. To Canada, I think.'

Tom frowned. No one got out of the game. A bullet, the courts or drugs took them out of the game but no one ever got to just leave. 'Was this before or after Rose married Gerry?'

Scanlan scratched the shadow on his chin as he thought about it. 'It would have been before. Yes, definitely before. I remember now that the wedding was a big affair and the baby came along soon after.'

'You mean she was pregnant before they got married?' Tom asked.

'Duh!' Shay rolled his eyes.

Tom stared out the window. He could not understand what had attracted a woman like Rose to Gerry O'Dowd. Maybe she had been drunk and gone to bed with him. Did she only marry him because she got pregnant? She may not have known the kind of man he was or what he was capable of. But then, once she realised, why had she stayed with him? Had he forced her too? Is that why she had said her life was beginning? He could not forget those words, or her smile when she said them, no matter how much he wanted to.

At the station, Superintendent Flynn paced around the incident room with his hands behind his back. 'It seems an open and shut case. The witness is the office manager from the doctor's surgery across the road. She couldn't be more solid.' He stopped in front of Inspector Davis. 'Refresh our memories, Inspector?'

Davis looked down at his notebook and read out the witness statement. 'I heard a screech of breaks and a scream and I ran to the door. I saw a motorbike. The driver and pillion passenger were dressed completely in black. The passenger pointed a handgun at a man who was on the pavement outside the post office and said, "A message from Mossie." The man started running but the pair on the bike went after him. The passenger fired five or six shots. I called the doctor out of the surgery and we tried to help him but he was dead before the ambulance arrived.'

Tom shook his head and sighed.

Flynn's beady gaze landed on him. 'Something you want to share, Doyle?' he demanded.

'It's too easy and it's just not Mossie's style. He never sends messages. He has never needed to and he is not stupid. This case stinks, Superintendent. Someone is setting him up.'

'You think that someone would risk pissing off one of the most powerful drug families in the county just to get at Maher?'

Tom shook his head. 'I don't have the answers, sir. I'm just saying that I find it very hard to believe that Mossie Maher is our man.'

Flynn glared at him. 'Then find out who is.' He looked around the room at the officers. 'But let me make myself perfectly clear. I don't want any cock-ups. I want everything checked and double-checked. I don't want any loose talk in the pub or tip-offs to journalists. We are going to nail Maher.' His eyes met Tom's. 'Or whoever the guilty party is. Doyle, contact the boys in Limerick and tell them to bring Maher in, then get down there first thing and question him. Bannon, get the official statements from any witnesses. Davis, keep on top of the door-to-door enquiries. Set up a road block tomorrow at the same time the murder took place in case anyone driving past noticed anything. Mulvey, O'Donnell, we need to track down that bike and get hold of all CCTV footage in the area. Report back to me at noon tomorrow.'

'Yes, boss.' The officers began to leave but Tom didn't move.

Scanlan's eyes flicked between Tom and Flynn. 'Do you want me to call the boys in Limerick?'

'Yes. Then go home and get some sleep and pick me up at six,' Tom said.

'Right so. Goodnight.' Scanlan left them alone.

'My office, Doyle. Now,' Flynn said and strode from the room.

Tom took the seat in front of Flynn's desk. The superintendent didn't look up. He just started to read the file in front of him.

'Joined the Gardaí straight from school. Excelled at the entrance exam and basically top of the class throughout his studies. A dependable and dedicated Garda. Joined the drug squad three years ago.' He glanced up at Tom. 'Your previous superintendents are full of praise, but they agree that you can be stubborn and headstrong.'

'I wouldn't say that,' Tom protested. 'It's just when I get a feeling in my gut I have to follow it up.'

'And your gut is telling you to ignore this evidence?' The superintendent shook his head and sighed. 'Look, Tom, it's dreadful what happened to your partner but you can't let that colour how you do your job. Have you lost your nerve? Is that what this is about? Can you not face the man?'

Tom closed his eyes and counted to ten. When he felt in control again he looked directly into Flynn's eyes. 'With respect, sir, don't you think I would love to see Maher locked up? But I know how the man operates and I am convinced he is innocent. By focusing on Maher I'm afraid we are going to miss something much bigger. Perhaps there is someone new on the scene.' He put Rose firmly to the back of his mind.

Flynn looked at him for a long moment. 'I have a press conference to give. Maher is our main suspect until you can find a better one. Is that understood?'

'Of course.' Tom stood up and went to the door.

'Doyle?'

He looked back and he felt sick at the pity he saw in Flynn's eyes.

'If you would prefer I can send someone else to Limerick.'

'No, sir. I'll take care of it.'

Chapter Four

Tom was grateful that Scanlan wasn't a talker. His head was throbbing thanks to the half bottle of Jameson he'd knocked back the night before as he went over the case in his mind. The stuffy car was making him sleepy and the motion had his stomach churning. 'Take the turn off for Borris, I need coffee,' he ordered.

In the gents' loo, Tom washed his hands and splashed water over his face and neck before realising there was no towel. 'Damn,' he muttered. He used his thick hair to dry his hands, turning his tousled mane dark. Slicked-back, and with his brown eyes looking almost black from lack of sleep, he looked like his father. He leaned heavily on the sink. How he would like to talk to the old man now. His father was a former Garda, and Tom had always enjoyed discussing cases with him. They often disagreed, but his dad could always make him think. Susie, his late partner at work, had done the same. But now they were both gone. He had been very sad when his dad died, naturally, but he had felt a whole range of emotions about Susie's death, guilt being the main one.

After she died, the Gardaí wanted him to get counselling before returning to work. He had gone reluctantly to a very nice woman for an hour, once a week, for two months. Not that it helped, and she knew it. She had wanted him to take a desk job for a year but he would have quit before he would be chained to a desk. And so, the powers that be had put their heads together and came up with the idea of transferring him to Dublin. Tom jumped at the offer.

The flat he had moved into when his marriage broke up had been cold and lifeless, which was how he had felt. It was a far cry from the comfortable home his wife Julia had created for them. It was a home where they had planned to raise their family. When Julia told him that she was pregnant, he scooped her up and swung her around in delight until he realised that she was as stiff as a board in his arms. He set her back on her feet and stared into her face. Was there a problem with the pregnancy? Was she sick? Tom was taken aback to see that her expression was one of irritation and annoyance.

'How could you even think I would want a child at a time like this?' she demanded. She had just been promoted and she was only twenty-five. 'There is plenty of time for children later,' she said tearfully. At first, they discussed it calmly. Then the arguments and accusations started, broken only by cold, tense silences, the air almost vibrating with anger. It had been almost a relief when she told him she was off to a conference in London for a few days. God, how had he swallowed that one? When she came home he knew as soon as he looked in her eyes that she had had a termination. Without a word, he had gone up to their bedroom and started packing. She followed him and stood watching, stunned.

'Why are you leaving me?' Julia wept. She said that they were made for each other and some day they would have a family, just not right now. But

Tom had known that he would never be able to forgive her and left without looking back. They say tragedy comes in threes. It certainly had for him. He had lost his partner, his child and his wife within a few months. The move to Dublin was like a lifeline.

He hadn't spent much time in the capital in the past, but had always enjoyed his visits. He rented a small, cosy house in Santry that had been built in the fifties. It was halfway between the station and the city. Perfect. He had felt almost positive at this second chance, but it seemed that he could not escape Limerick.

'What's this guy Maher like?' Scanlan asked as Tom stirred three sugars into his coffee.

He thought about it for a few moments before answering. How did you sum up the evil of Mossie Maher? He forced himself to think about the man without emotion, as if he had not changed Tom's life forever. 'He's in his late sixties. He's married to the same woman for years but he has always played away too. He gets off on violence, without doubt. He seems to take pleasure in making people suffer. But any crime we have been able to pin on him was nowhere near as clean and tidy as Gerry O'Dowd's murder. I'd say he has a heart of ice, only I'm not convinced he has a heart at all.'

'Is he a druggie?'

'No, like the youngest O'Dowd . . .' he frowned as he tried to recall the name.

'Jude,' Scanlan said.

'Yes, Jude. They seem like two of a kind. Muck everyone else up, reap the rewards and enjoy the floorshow. Anyway, in the unlikely event that the Super is right, we need to check if anyone has been moving in on Maher's territory. Have there been any strange crimes recently? Has Maher been behaving more strangely than usual? We need to follow every lead. It's the only way that we can move on and find O'Dowd's real killer.'

'No problem. Want me to do that while you interview Maher?'

'No, I'd like you to meet him. I want to get your take on the man. I have a bit of private business to attend to before we leave Limerick, so you can have a natter with the lads at the station while I'm gone.'

'Visiting family?' Scanlan asked.

'No, just some friends.'

Shay looked up from his coffee. 'How long were you and Susie Macken partners?'

Tom froze. Hearing her name out loud came as a shock. It had been a while.

Scanlan looked at him. 'Hey, sorry, if you don't want to talk about it—'

'It's okay. We were together for just over two years.'

'It was a car accident, right?'

'It was no accident,' Tom said. 'One of Maher's thugs ran her off the road.' Tom focused on a mother trying to strap a cooing baby into a high chair. He was reminded of Toby and Rose, and of Julia, and the happiness she had taken from him. 'It was a dark night. The road was wet and it was a bad bend and there were no witnesses. But Susie knew that road like the back of her hand. She was on her way home to her husband and kids.'

'Bloody hell,' Scanlan muttered.

'It was Maher's work alright. We had a tip-off earlier in the week and raided a farmhouse. We found a stash of cocaine worth a couple of million. We couldn't link it to Maher. He is good at covering his tracks. People are either too afraid of him or too dependent on him to snitch. But we were happy enough to have put a dent in his wallet and keep the stuff off the streets. My mistake was in stopping by to gloat. You don't do something like that with Mossie and get away with it. Susie's "accident" happened the next evening.'

'But why wouldn't he have taken *you* out?'

'He's a clever bastard. He knew he would do a lot more damage taking her out than me.'

Shay frowned. 'I don't understand.'

'I was mad as hell, grieving and feeling so bloody guilty. There was no way the Super was going to let me have any more to do with the drugs squad.'

'So he took the two of you out of the picture. Clever, fucker.' Scanlan met Tom's eyes. 'Does Flynn know this?'

'Sure.'

'And he's sending you back there?'

'He gave me the option to refuse but that would be madness. I know the man.' Tom finished his coffee.

'It's madness to go, if you ask me,' Shay said.

'Well, I'm not asking you. I told you, Mossie is not behind the O'Dowd shooting.' Tom shook his head. 'I would stake my life on it.'

Scanlan frowned. 'I really wish you hadn't said that.'

Chapter Five

Tom had his back slapped and his hand shaken when they arrived at the station in Limerick. But while he was joking with his old work mates, his stomach was churning. The hardest part was when he walked into the office he had shared with five other officers and saw Susie's old desk. He knew that it was going to be hard coming back here, but not *this* hard. How would he sit in an interview room with the man who had destroyed the life of a wonderful woman, simply out of spite? He wanted to kill Maher with his bare hands, and slowly too. He wanted to see fear in his eyes and hear him beg for mercy. He wanted to watch as the life drained from the man's worthless body.

'The Super is ready for you,' the sergeant said from the doorway.

'Cheers, Liam.' He took his cup of coffee and made his way down the corridor towards his old super's office. The door was open and he knocked and went in.

Mick Cronan stood up and held out his hand, smiling. 'Tom, great to see you. How are you doing?'

'Good, thanks,' Tom said, sitting on the windowsill as he had always done.

Mick sat back in his chair and looked at him. 'Is this a good idea?' No small talk, no messing about. That's one of the things Tom had always liked about the man. So many superintendents loved the sound of their own voices.

Denis Flynn, for one. Mick just wanted to get the job done.

'I was sent here to question Mossie and I'll do it,' Tom said.

'I read about the case. It doesn't sound like Maher's style,' Mick remarked.

'I agree, but the witness heard the shooter say, "A present from Mossie," so we have to follow it up. Any reason at all why someone would want to set Maher up?'

'Thousands,' Mick said.

'True. But why would someone want to stir up trouble between the two gangs? They're not even in the same territory. It doesn't make sense.'

'Ah, the definition of territory has changed, lad. These days there is as much business being done online as there is on the street. Maybe more.'

It kept coming back to the internet, Tom thought. Perhaps that is why he felt frustrated by this case. He wasn't comfortable with technology. He doubted that Mossie was either. But Jude was. 'The youngest O'Dowd is a computer whizz kid,' he told Mick. 'He's never done time. They can't find a thing on him but there doesn't seem to be any doubt that he is in it up to his neck. Maybe *he* is the brains behind the operation.'

'If he is then he will be thinking the same way we are. That this is a set-up.'

'And he will probably know who is doing it and why. Jesus, this could be the start of a very bloody war,' Tom said.

'It could.' Mick glanced at the clock. 'Come on, let's go see the man himself. We've had him here a few hours now. He should be tired and just about pissed off enough to talk.'

Tom stood up. 'Just let me take a leak and I'll be right with you.'

He barely made it to the stall before he threw up. He stood with his back to the door, trying to get his breathing under control. He wiped his mouth with toilet paper and flushed it down the loo. Outside, he washed his hands, rinsed his mouth and took out a stick of gum. He looked at his white face in the mirror. He could not show any weakness or temper in front of Mossie. He chewed the gum and made his way back down the corridor to Mick's office. 'Ready when you are, sir.'

Mossie looked anything but tired or ruffled when they joined him and Scanlan in the interview room. Even though he was a small man he had the body of an athlete. Strong, iron-grey hair was brushed back from a high forehead, and his sallow skin did not go with his name or nationality. He wore a sharp grey suit. If someone walked into the interview room, Tom figured they would think Mossie was the detective, and he, in his black fleece and jeans, was the crook. Only the cold eyes and thin lips hinted that this was someone you didn't mess with. How many deaths had Mossie been responsible for? Deaths that they didn't know about and maybe never would?

Tom and the superintendent took the seats opposite Maher and, after a nod from Mick, Scanlan pressed the record button.

'Second of August, 2013, 9.50am. Interview with Mr Mossie Maher. Officers present, Superintendent Michael Cronan, Detective Inspector Tom Doyle and Inspector Shay Scanlan.'

'DI Doyle, what a pleasure. I thought you had moved on,' Maher said coolly.

Tom met his gaze but said nothing. He saw a flicker of irritation in Mossie's eyes. Good.

The superintendent questioned him while Tom watched the criminal's reactions. Mossie was just as aware of him. While Mick was asking the questions, it was Tom that Mossie watched, a slight smile on his thin lips. Tom found it unnerving but he tried not to show it. Mossie's eyes dropped to the pen Tom was rolling between his fingers and his smile got wider.

Bastard! Tom wanted to rip his head off. He put down the pen, sat back in his chair and crossed his arms. He could feel sweat trickle between his shoulder blades. He was glad he wasn't in a shirt. How Mossie would love to see him all hot and bothered.

Mick fired questions but Maher batted them away like irritating flies. He claimed he was having lunch with a friend at the time of the murder. He rattled off the name of a restaurant that was part of a club he owned. But he didn't need an alibi. No one thought he had carried out the hit himself. He would have just made a call or sent an email. Tom scribbled a note and put it in front of the Super.

Did we get a search warrant?

The superintendent nodded and scribbled back, *Raiding his place right now.*

'Why on earth would I kill O'Dowd?' Mossie said, seeming to tire of the game. 'He's nothing to me. You're just using this as an excuse to search my house and I'm sure that's not legal when I could not possibly be a suspect.' He started to stand up. 'I've had enough of this—'

'Sit,' the Super glared at him.

'We have a witness. The shooter said, "A present from Mossie",' Tom said watching closely and there was no mistaking the surprise and disbelief in the man's eyes.

'Nonsense,' he laughed.

Tom shook his head. 'Fact. Why do you think I'm here? You are our main suspect, Mossie. Unless you can tell us why someone would want to set you up.'

There was a flicker of doubt in Maher's eyes and then the shutters came down. He gave Tom a cold smile. 'Call my solicitor. I'm not saying another word until he gets here.'

The interview was halted and Tom left Scanlan with some of the lads on the drugs squad. He drove out of the car park and headed out of the city, feeling bad tempered and unsettled. When he rounded the bend on the quiet country road, he pulled over onto the grass and stared at the spot where Susie's car had gone off the road. He got out and walked across the road. It was a lovely sunny day. Where the mud and skid marks had been was now a field of green. He would never forget that awful night when he got the call. He had driven like a mad man, arriving at the scene just as the lads were taping off the area.

The car had been on its side at the bottom of the incline. He had hurried, slipping and sliding in the mud, feeling his way through the dark to the lights around the accident scene. He had known that Susie was dead as soon as he saw the paramedics standing around talking. He had joined them, putting off the moment when he would have to face reality.

How was he going to break the news to her husband, Pete, and the girls? He had been tempted to leave it to another officer but he could almost hear Susie's teasing voice, her eyes twinkling, saying 'Chicken!' No, he owed it to her. It was the very least he could do. When he had finally turned and started towards the vehicle, a uniform officer stepped into his path.

'Sorry, Tom, but forensics haven't been here yet.'

'I won't touch anything.' He went to step past the guard but the hand on his arm stopped him.

'It's really not a good idea.'

'She was my partner,' he said, looking the young lad in the eye. The hand dropped.

He had seen plenty of road traffic accents and murder scenes, but none had involved someone he loved. And, yes, he had loved Susie. She was the big sister he never had. As he neared the vehicle and saw the bloody mess that was his partner, he did something he had never done before in his life. He fainted.

When he came to, he was propped up against a tree. A paramedic crouched beside him. 'Are you okay?'

He nodded and refused the offer of a lift home. He wanted to stay until forensics had finished their job. His cheeks wet with tears, Tom had watched them lift her lifeless body into a body bag and take it away in an unmarked van.

Tom shook his head to rid himself of the images and went back to the car. It was only a short drive to the small estate where Pete and his children lived. He half hoped they weren't at home. He felt overcome with guilt every time he looked into the girls' eyes, despite the fact that he only saw love there. But his hopes were dashed as soon as he got out of the car. A small figure came hurtling towards him, wrapping her skinny arms around his legs.

'Uncle Tom!'

'Elsa!' He lifted her above his head, making her giggle. She was wearing a princess dress and grubby pink ballet shoes. A tiara sat lopsided on her curly dark hair. 'Are you going to a party?' he asked as he put her down.

She frowned up at him. 'No, why?'

He laughed. 'No reason.'

She took his hand and tugged him towards the house. 'Daddy! Alice!'

Pete came to the door, a dish cloth in his hand, and smiled. 'Tom, this is a nice surprise.'

Tom shook the man's hand, noting the dark circles under his eyes, and the way his jeans hung loose on his hips. 'I'm only down for the day. Work,' he explained. 'I thought I'd drop in and say hello.'

'Elsa, run and find your sister. Coffee or a beer?' he asked Tom.

'Coffee would be lovely.' Tom followed him into the sunny room where he had eaten countless times with Susie's family. 'How are the girls doing?'

'They're doing really well.' Pete put on the kettle and spooned coffee into two mugs.

'And you?' Tom asked.

'Fine. Everyone has been great. The girls have so many invitations to sleep-overs and play dates I hardly see them. My mother and Susie's folks spend a lot of time here. And you? How is Dublin?'

Tom took the mug Pete offered him. 'It's good. Different.'

Pete gave him a knowing look. 'So the girls are grand, I'm grand and you're grand.'

Tom laughed. 'It's the pits really, isn't it?'

'The pits,' Pete agreed. 'I still can't believe she's gone. I keep expecting her to walk in the door. I see her everywhere. The number of times I've had to stop myself from saying to the girls, "Ask mammy".'

Tom nodded in understanding. He had found himself picking up the phone to call or text Susie many times. 'Maybe you should move,' he said. Pete was a cabinet maker who supplied a small number of exclusive shops. He could work from anywhere.

'God, no. I couldn't cope alone and it wouldn't be fair to take the girls from their grandparents and friends. They already lost their mother.' Pete gave him a stern look. 'And you.'

Tom looked away. It was true, he hadn't been back since the move to Dublin and he had only phoned a couple of times. He would have to make more of an effort.

'Uncle Tom!' Susie's eldest daughter came running into the kitchen and hugged him.

'Alice! How are you, sweetheart?'

She gave him a brave smile but her lovely brown eyes were sad. 'Okay. Are you home for good?'

'No. Sorry, I'm just down for the day.'

Her face fell. 'Oh.'

'You know what, Pete? I have two spare bedrooms. You and the girls will have to come and visit me in Dublin. There is *so* much to do there.'

Elsa had followed her sister into the room and now sat on the table swinging her legs. Her face lit up. 'Oh, yes, Daddy! We could go to the zoo and see the lions.'

'Please can we go?' Alice begged.

'If Tom is mad enough to take us on, who am I to say no?' Pete gave him a grateful smile.

Chapter Six

Driving back to the station, Tom opened the windows and took some deep breaths. Shay had called to say that Maher's solicitor had arrived and the interview could continue. Having seen Susie's family, Tom was going to find it even harder not to kill the bastard. He wondered at himself and why he was working so hard to convince everyone that Mossie wasn't guilty. Did it matter? Wouldn't it be good to see him go down for something he hadn't done? Wouldn't it be justice for Susie? The last thing he wanted was for the spotlight to turn on Rose. Her words still haunted him but he did not believe she was capable of murder.

There was something else going on here. If only he could figure a link between the O'Dowds and Maher. He realised he was quite close to Mossie's house. On impulse he turned off and drove down the country road to Mossie's eye-catching bungalow. The grounds were walled and gated. He noted the cameras tucked behind one of the pillars. The electric gates were open and Tom wasn't surprised to see a Garda car parked next to Mossie's Volvo estate.

'Tom!' The guard at the door looked surprised to see him.

'Hello, PJ. I'm down to interview Mossie about the O'Dowd killing. Have you found anything interesting?'

The man shook his head in disgust. 'Do we ever? The lads are just packing up all the computer equipment to take back to the station. Mossie's wife is giving them dog's abuse.'

Tom had to laugh. Dolly Maher was a force to be reckoned with. He couldn't understand why she had stood by Mossie all these years. She had to know about all his other women. She didn't need a man to look after her. She was well able to look after herself. Maybe it suited her to enjoy a comfortable life and turn a blind eye to his cheating and dark side. Maybe she just didn't care. 'I think I will say a quick hello. It would be rude not to.' Tom winked.

The guard grinned and stood back to let him pass. He found the other guards in Mossie's study. Dolly stood with her arms crossed and a cigarette dangling from her mouth. She turned as he walked in, clearly surprised to see him.

'Mrs Maher.' He nodded. 'Sorry about the bother.'

Her pencilled brows raised. 'Really?'

If Tom were to sum up Dolly Maher in one word, that word would be 'hard'. Her features were hard, her voice was hard and her eyes were hard. He found it impossible to imagine her crying, or being soft, tender or loving. What had happened to turn her into this harsh, angry woman? Was it something Mossie had done to her? Was it just the vital armour of a criminal's wife?

'What are you doing here? I thought you moved to Dublin,' she demanded.

'I'm just visiting. Can I have five minutes?'

Dolly gave a curt nod and led the way out to the kitchen. She picked up a mug of coffee and leaned back against the counter. 'I was sorry to hear about your partner,' she muttered.

He searched her eyes for sarcasm or cruelty, but her expression was blank. 'Thanks.' He sat down at the table and took out his notebook and pen. 'You know the reason your husband was arrested?' he asked.

'Yes. Has he been charged?'

He tried to judge her tone of voice. It certainly did not sound worried or angry. If anything it was carefully neutral. 'No. We have strong evidence against him but he claims he had nothing to do with the murder. He says that he is being framed. Any idea who would want to set him up?'

'No.' Her eyes were sharp. 'Now why are you *really* here, Detective?'

He watched Dolly stub out the cigarette and light up a fresh one. Was he making her nervous? That would be a first. He noticed a hotel flier on the table and picked it up. 'Off on holiday?' he asked casually.

'Just back from a health spa.' Dolly pulled on her fag.

'Oh, really? I've never been to one. I'm told they are a great place to relax.' He pretended to study the flyer, thinking that the spa had not worked on Dolly. She looked anything but relaxed. 'Not sure I could afford this on my salary. Mossie must be selling a lot of . . . cars.' Mossie's 'official' business was flogging Toyotas.

'It's an anniversary present.'

'How many years are you married now?'

'Thirty-five.'

'That's a long time. Nice one. What's the secret to staying with one person so long?'

She pressed her lips together in a thin smile. 'Tolerance. She looked at her watch. 'Your time is running out, Detective.'

'Oh, right. Sorry. Just one more thing. Where were you between twelve and three o'clock yesterday afternoon?'

She looked completely floored by the question but paused only a second before answering. 'I was at a family funeral.'

He watched her and, for once, saw real emotion in her eyes. 'Sorry for your trouble.'

'Your five minutes are up, Detective.' She turned away. 'It's my husband you arrested. Go and question him and leave me in peace.'

'Will do. Goodbye, Mrs Maher.'

They got little more out of Mossie and by seven o'clock Tom and Scanlan were on their way home. They had got an extension so Maher could be held for another few hours but no one expected him to cooperate.

'Bloody frustrating day,' Scanlan muttered, drumming his fingers on the steering wheel. 'It would take weeks to break that bastard down and get to the truth.'

'Or maybe for once he is telling the truth and he is innocent.' Tom was beginning to think that there was a link between the two families on opposite sides of the country. Dolly had been more nervous than he'd ever seen her. 'Find out whose funeral Dolly Maher attended yesterday. She said it was family, and yet Mossie was at a lunch meeting. Odd?'

Shay nodded. 'I'll check it out.'

'I might pay another visit to the sad widow.'

'Rose?' Scanlan glanced across at him. 'Why?'

Tom shrugged. 'Why not?'

Scanlan sniggered. 'Well, I suppose she *is* single.'

Chapter Seven

Tom looked up at the clock. This meeting had gone on for nearly two hours. He had learned nothing new other than they had two more witnesses, who had heard the fateful words laying the blame firmly at Mossie's door.

His mind wandered to Rose. In the end, he had waited until the morning after the funeral to drop by. He figured that there was more chance of getting her alone. And he was right. Toby was gone to the park to play with his cousins.

Rose was in a silk wrap when she opened the door. It was after eleven. She knotted the belt around her waist and invited him in. He looked around and saw curtains twitching in the house across the road.

'I better not,' he said, leaning against the front door.

'Shouldn't you have a minder with you?' She glanced at the empty car.

He felt himself blush. 'I should.'

She looked into his eyes and smiled. 'I need some baby food. Let me get dressed and you can drop me at the shops. We can talk on the way.'

He waited in the car, glad one of them had their wits about them. It was madness coming here alone. Anything she told him would not be allowed in evidence. But then he didn't really want to talk about the case. He wanted to know more about her and how she'd ended up with O'Dowd. He could fool himself that he was just trying to find out if the two brothers got on. Try to find out who would step into Gerry's shoes. The truth was he just wanted to see her again. Minutes later a door banged and he looked up to see Rose walking towards him. She was dressed simply, in blue jeans, a black top and flat black pumps. Her hair was pinned up off her face. She looked beautiful. When she sat in next to him and smiled it was all he could do to tear his eyes away and start the car.

'Is Toby okay?' he asked, trying to concentrate. All he could think about was how the perfume she wore was light and sweet, nothing like Dolly's strong, heavy scent.

'He's fine. Everyone is making such a fuss over him he hasn't even asked about Gerry.'

'That's good, I suppose.' But Tom found it depressing that a father could be forgotten so quickly.

She seemed to sense what he was thinking. 'Gerry wasn't home much. It wasn't safe for him to have a set routine.'

'So he felt his life was in danger?'

'Everyone who gets into the drugs business puts their lives at risk,' she said with a scornful note in her voice.

'But your brother got out alive,' he said.

She stiffened. 'Ronan was nothing like them. He had a problem for a while but he got help.'

'And he's living in Canada?

'I'm not sure, we don't keep in touch.' She looked at him. 'Why are you so interested in my brother?'

'I'm not really, I just wondered how you came to meet Gerry and I'm guessing it was through Ronan.'

'Yes,' she said, turning her head away. 'I really don't want to talk about it, Detective. That part of my life is over.'

'Sure. Sorry.' He noted the change in her attitude.

'You can pull in anywhere here.' She pointed at the bus stop across the road from the shops. It was clear she wanted to get away from him.

'Rose.' He put a hand on her arm. 'It may not be so easy to walk away. If you have any problems, call me.' He held out his card.

She ignored it and stepped onto the pavement. 'I'll be fine. Thanks for the lift.' She crossed the road and did not look back.

Tom tuned back in to the briefing, his gaze drawn to the whiteboard at the top of the room. He studied the photos of Gerry O'Dowd's body. Three freeze-frames from the post office, pharmacy and bank CCTV showed blurred shots of the motorbike driving away. The passenger's arm outstretched, his gun clearly on view.

'Doyle?'

He looked up at the superintendent. 'Sir?'

'Talk to Jude O'Dowd and see what he has to say.'

Tom was curious to meet Jude. It was important that he get to know the criminals that would become a regular feature of his day. He snapped his folder shut and stood up. 'I'm on it,' he said, thankful to be getting away from the Super and the stuffy meeting room.

The youngest O'Dowd had a mop of red hair and frameless glasses sat on plump cheeks. He looked more like a cheeky schoolboy than a gangster. Jude spoke in a clear voice with no accent thanks to the posh school he had attended, unlike his big brothers. He greeted the detectives in a polite and friendly manner and led them in to a large, modern kitchen. He sat down at the table. 'You have to excuse me, I was in the middle of a meal. Help yourself to tea.' He waved at the mugs on the worktop.

'No thanks.' Tom took the chair opposite and watched the man tuck into a huge fry-up. A tower of toast sat on a plate by his side. Scanlan leaned against the large American fridge, trying to hide a grin.

'Sorry to bother you at this difficult time,' Tom said. 'You must be devastated at the death of your brother.'

'The murder,' Jude corrected between mouthfuls.

'Yes, indeed. Our prime suspect at the moment is Mossie Maher. Do you know him?'

'Never met the bastard.' Jude stuffed a rasher into his gob.

Tom watched him closely. From what he had been told, the two men didn't need to meet to do business. 'Did Gerry know him?'

'No idea.'

'Any idea why Mossie would have wanted him dead?'

'No.' He took a slug of tea.

'Did Gerry have any other enemies that you think might have been responsible?'

Jude met his eyes. 'I'm sure that Detective Scanlan has already told you that my family has many enemies.'

Tom held his gaze, wondering what was going on inside this guy's head. He didn't seem interested in the case or upset about his brother's death. Well, it wasn't putting him off his grub anyway. Was it all an act? Tom felt weary. Dublin was proving to be as frustrating as Limerick. These feckers were a law unto themselves. He stood up. 'Thanks for your time.'

Jude looked up in surprise.

Tom turned back in the doorway just the way Columbo had. 'Oh, how's your sister-in-law doing?' Jude looked rattled. Tom felt a tingle of excitement. 'Rose?'

'Well, she's devastated of course,' Jude muttered.

Tom nodded and looked at Scanlan. 'We must drop in and let her know how the case is progressing.'

'She's not at home.'

'Where is she? In case we need to get a hold of her,' Tom said.

Jude scowled. 'Why would you need her? She's the victim. You have your killer.'

'We don't know that,' Scanlan said. 'Where is she, Jude?'

The man muttered the name of a posh hotel in the midlands. Tom tried to hide his surprise. This was a bolt from the blue.

'What?' Scanlan asked when they were in the car.

'Nothing.' Tom wasn't sure why, but he felt it best to keep his thoughts to himself for the moment. They didn't make sense anyway, nothing did. Could it really be just chance that Dolly and Rose went to the same spa? It was not Rose's first time. The slippers she wore were the same as the type worn by the woman in the flier. They had the hotel name on the front.

He had not made the link until now. But so what if they both went to this fancy place? Their husbands were rich drug lords. Was it any wonder their wives hung out in a place that would have top security? And even if they had met at the hotel, they wouldn't have been drawn to each other. Two more different women you couldn't meet. But then Tom thought of what Rose had said the night of Gerry's murder, 'Today my life begins.' Was she behind Gerry's murder? Had she asked Dolly to get Mossie to take him out?

His thoughts were interrupted by a call coming in on his mobile. He checked the screen and saw it was Mick Cronan in Limerick.

'Super?'

'We just got word from IT forensics. They took Mossie's PC apart and found substantial evidence that he was behind O'Dowd's murder. He has just been charged.'

Chapter Eight

His phone beeped and Tom picked it up to check the text. It was Shay wondering what was keeping him. He sat back in his chair, put his feet on the desk and stared up at the noticeboard. It was covered with photos, clippings and the notes he'd made as he tried to work out who had *really* killed Gerry O'Dowd. But it looked like he was wrong.

The team had gone for a drink to celebrate the end of the case but Tom couldn't face it. Maher was going down for ordering Gerry's murder, but they still didn't have the culprits. The bike had been stolen and was found a few miles away, burned out. Despite tons of CCTV footage, none of it showed anyone known to the guards. Tom had asked Mick Cronan what Mossie's reaction had been when they confronted him with the messages they found on his laptop. Mick said that the criminal had looked stunned. So if it was a surprise to Maher, that ruled out Tom's theory that Rose had asked him to take care of her husband. Could Dolly have organised it? That didn't make sense. She would not have let Mossie take the rap for it. Not after sticking by him for thirty-five years. Which left Gerry's beautiful wife.

Tom had watched Rose O'Dowd carefully when they had gone to tell her Maher had been charged, but she had barely reacted. She had seemed not to care. Either she knew nothing or she was a damn good actress. God, he hated to think that this woman might be no better than her husband, that she might have had something to do with his murder.

But he was sure that Maher was innocent. If Dolly and Rose were too, that meant there was someone new in town. Someone who could be more dangerous than O'Dowd and Maher. Someone clever enough to take out the two biggest players in the country at once. Jude O'Dowd, perhaps? Had there been trouble between the brothers? Had he been so keen to take over that he had used Mossie to clear the way? He was certainly smart enough to do it. What Tom knew about computers could be written on a beer mat, but he suspected that planting false information on Mossie's laptop would not be that difficult for someone like Jude.

He glanced back up at the board and thought of all these loose ends that his bosses seemed to want to ignore. He could see the reason why. Mossie had been set up and handed to them on a plate. It was hard to resist the chance to lock up the man responsible for the vast drug problem in the south west for more than twenty years. Did it matter that Maher might be innocent of this crime, when he had been guilty of so many others?

His house had been raided many times. They had taken all his computer equipment and phones every time and never found a thing. Why this time? And then there was the funeral that Dolly had attended on the day Gerry O'Dowd had been shot. It turned out it was her niece who had taken her own life. It was very strange that Mossie hadn't been there to support his wife at such a sad time. But the bit that troubled

Tom the most was about Rose O'Dowd's brother, Ronan. He was supposed to be in Canada, but Scanlan had not been able to trace him. They hadn't followed it up in the end. Forensics had all the evidence needed to convict Mossie, but it was bugging Tom.

His thoughts turned to Rose, as they so often did. What was going on in that beautiful head? God, he had it bad. This was daft. Even if she was totally innocent, how could he hunger for a woman who had married into the O'Dowd family? How could she live with what they were, what they did? How could she look at her son knowing that he could end up just like them? Yet Tom clung on to the fact that she clearly adored Toby. She was a good person, he was sure of it. Or did he just need her to be? His eyes returned to the noticeboard and the two lines he had underlined in red marker. He had put big question marks beside them. The funeral Dolly Maher had been to and Rose O'Dowd's brother.

It was no use, he couldn't let it go. Grabbing his jacket and car keys he marched out of his office and down the corridor. He was going back to his old patch to get some answers.

He was near Limerick when a snitch of his, a Dubliner, called him.

'Hey, Detective, you were looking for me?'

'I was Milo, just needed some info on a lad that got caught up in the Dublin scene. I thought you might know him. The word is he did a bit of selling for the O'Dowds. Ronan Fitzgerald is his name.'

'The toff. Ah, yeah, I remember him. He didn't last long.'

'I heard he got out and started a new life.'

Milo laughed. 'The only life he started was in the next world, boss.'

Tom shook his head. So Rose's brother was dead? Did she know? 'Did Gerry O'Dowd have him killed?'

'One of them got him. Who knows or cares which? Evil bastards, the lot of them.'

'Okay, thanks, Milo. I'll see you around.'

'No bother, boss. Don't do anything I wouldn't do.' He laughed and hung up.

The news didn't come as much of a surprise. It had seemed a bit far-fetched to him from the start, but if Rose knew Ronan was dead, it gave her a motive.

He phoned Scanlan, who answered after a few rings. He sounded pissed.

'We were wondering where you had got to. Are you on your way? Come on and get a few pints into you.'

'Not going to make it, Shay, sorry. Something has come up. Personal stuff. I'm on my way to Limerick. Do me a favour. Let the Super know I might not make it in tomorrow.'

Scanlan laughed. 'I don't think many of us will be in tomorrow. But don't worry, I'll give him the message.'

'Cheers, Shay. Have one for me,' Tom said and rung off.

When he walked into the coffee shop at seven the next morning, Joan, another Guard he had worked with, was already there. She stood up and they hugged. They ordered breakfast and he gave her a sheepish smile. 'I'm very grateful for this.'

'You should be,' she said. 'My shift doesn't start until twelve. I'm not that keen on helping to get Mossie Maher off the hook.'

She had been Susie's best friend. They had started in the Force together and she too was convinced that Mossie had been behind Susie's death.

'I know that, Joan. It's just a few loose ends I'd like to tie up before I move on to the next case. You know what I mean?'

She nodded. 'Sure. Fire away.'

'Tell me what you know about Dolly Maher's niece.'

'Ah, poor Linda,' Joan sighed. 'You know that she's dead?'

'Yes. Suicide. Any idea why?'

'That poor girl always had problems. She drank and took drugs from a very young age. She also seemed paranoid. She came to us a few times, terrified. She said someone was trying to hurt her. But once we poured coffee into her and calmed her down she would decide that she was fine and be out the door in a flash.'

'Was she married?'

'No. Sure she was only nineteen.'

Tom was shocked. 'I didn't realise.' He could kick himself for not following up on this story before now. Dolly was in her sixties, so he had assumed the niece would be at least thirty.

'Was she still living with her parents?'

'No, there was never a father on the scene. Her mother died when she was very young. Dolly was her legal guardian. She went to live with them but it didn't work out.'

'Why not?' Tom felt the hairs stand up on the back of his neck.

'I think she was just too much for them. They didn't know how to handle her. Eventually Dolly packed her off to a cousin outside the city, to get her away from the booze and drugs.'

'But I've known Mossie for years. How come I didn't know about the niece?'

'She would have moved out by the time you joined the branch,' Joan said.

'And you know what families are like. It was all kept very quiet. Dolly made sure of that. It was only in the last year that Linda appeared on our radar again.'

'Why?'

'She was back in the city and more strung out than ever.'

'Was she living with Dolly?'

'I'm not sure.'

He mulled over what she had told him and thought about the timing of events. 'Did you know that Mossie wasn't at the funeral?'

Joan stared at him. 'No, I didn't! That's odd. I would have been there myself only I was off that week.'

'Makes you wonder, doesn't it? Could it be that Uncle Mossie was the one feeding her drug habit?'

'No, Dolly would not have allowed that. She would kill him first.'

Tom looked her in the eye. 'Only if she knew.'

He left Joan, his head reeling with this new information. Now he had two women with possible motives for getting rid of their husbands. Was it really just chance that Gerry was murdered the day of Linda's funeral? There had to be a link, he was sure of it. Why wasn't Mossie there? He always had an alibi but they were easily bought. But where had he been instead? Certainly not in Dublin shooting Gerry O'Dowd.

There was only one way Tom. could think of to get to the truth. It would mean taking a risk, one that both Flynn and Cronan would not be happy about. But he was back in Limerick and his gut was telling him what to do and this time, by God, he was going to do it.

There was silence when he buzzed the intercom at the gate and announced himself. For a moment he thought Dolly Maher might not let him in. She answered, her voice clipped. 'I should have known you would be back.'

The gates started to open and Tom drove in.

She was standing in the doorway, cigarette in hand, when he pulled up outside the house. 'Haven't you got him locked up? What more do you want? The house has been torn apart. There is nothing left to take.'

'I'm not here about the Gerry O'Dowd case.' He could see surprise in her eyes but no fear or anger. She seemed empty. He supposed she was grieving. He felt a moment's guilt for taking advantage of that. But, not one to look a gift horse in the mouth, when she turned and led the way to the kitchen, Tom followed.

'I wanted to ask you about Linda.' He could see her hand shake as she took a deep drag on the cigarette.

'What about her?'

'I had no idea of the events of her death, or that she was so young. I'm so very sorry. It must have been a dreadful shock.'

She swallowed hard and bowed her head. 'It was.'

'You were close?'

'She was my late sister's only child. Of course we were close.' Dolly turned away from him and stared out across the fields.

'But she didn't live with you?' Tom pressed on.

'You know damn well she didn't. What is all this about, Detective?'

Tom hoped his gut feeling was right. 'Your sister must be spinning in her grave,' he said.

She spun around. 'What the hell does that mean?'

'Drinking and taking drugs when she was only, what, twelve? You were some guardian!'

She seemed to deflate before him, leaning against the counter for support. 'I did everything I could to help her. It wasn't my fault,' Dolly began. 'I—'

'Oh, please!' He kept up, sensing her weakness. 'Where does a kid get the cash and the opportunity to get her hands on drugs unless she's left to her own devices?' His heart went out to her but he ignored the voice in his head telling him to back off and glared at her.

Dolly ran a hand through her hair. 'She was never alone, *never*! Why didn't she talk to me? I would have fixed everything if only she had told me.'

He watched her intently. He could see how upset she was, how close he was to the truth. *Please don't let me mess this up,* Tom thought. 'Mossie gave her the drugs, Dolly, didn't he?'

'I didn't know.' It came out as almost a sob. 'I swear to God, I never knew a thing. How could he? She was just a little girl.'

Tom was stunned that she had broken down so easily and he was disgusted with Mossie. He knew the man was to blame for awful crimes but to corrupt a child, and one in his care, his own wife's niece. The sick bastard.

Dolly sank into a chair, looking tired and old. 'When her mother died, the poor child was so upset, she never stopped crying. I thought that once she settled in with us she would be okay. But she just cried and cried, all day and all night. There was no talking to her. So, one night, Mossie gave her something to calm her so that she'd sleep. He said it was a very mild sedative and I believed him,' she said bitterly. 'But I had no reason to doubt him. He had never done anything to hurt me. We always wanted a child but I couldn't have kids. I was broken-hearted to lose my sister but I saw minding Linda as a chance for Mossie and me to be parents. I was happy to see him taking such an interest in her, caring for her. He would take her out on jaunts. Just the two of them. They were so close.' Her face hardened. 'I didn't realise how close.'

He stared at her as he tried to get his head around what she was saying. 'He abused her?' he asked, shocked.

Silent tears rolled down her cheeks. 'He got her hooked and then denied her unless she . . . pleased him.'

'Bloody hell,' Tom said, completely thrown. Yes, his gut had told him there was something wrong here, but he hadn't been expecting this.

'I didn't know, honestly I didn't,' Dolly sobbed. 'But I knew the signs of addiction. I knew that I had to get her away from him. I waited until he went off on one of his golfing trips and I sent her to live with my cousin. She was a

real old maid, but I knew that Linda
would be safe with her. Una wouldn't
allow a drop of sherry in the house,
never mind drugs.'

'Mossie must have been furious
when he got home,' Tom said, hoping
the criminal's wife would keep talking.

'He may well have been but he never
said a word. I felt it was odd at the time.
When I think about it now, I wonder if
he was afraid that I knew everything
and might report him.'

'What about Linda?'

Dolly looked sad. 'She was no better.
I went to see her from time to time and
tried to talk to her or get her to talk to
someone but she didn't want to know.
You're right. Barbara, my sister, would
be disgusted with me. I let her and
Linda down.' The tears rolled down
Dolly's cheeks.

Tom sat down beside her. 'At least
you got her away from him. You got her

to safety,' he comforted the weeping woman.

Dolly shook her head. 'No, it was too late. I didn't realise how hooked she was. You know as well as I do, if you need a fix you will always find a way to get one. She inhaled anything in Una's house that she could get her hands on. She robbed her sedatives, pain killers and sleeping pills, but Una never noticed. Then she started to chat up the older lads in the school. She got them to buy booze and drugs for her.'

'But how did she pay for them?' he asked.

Dolly gave him a scornful look. 'How do you think?'

Tom was knocked for six. This was a horror story. 'How do you know all this?' he asked.

Dolly wiped her face on her sleeve and reached for her smokes. Her hands were shaking so much she couldn't even open the packet. Tom took it from her, gave her a cigarette and lit it.

'Una fell and broke her leg and had to go into a nursing home to recover. She refused to let Linda stay in the house alone. She didn't trust her. She was right, of course. At that stage, Linda would have sold everything Una had just for a fix. I went there and tried to persuade her to come home with me but she fought me every step of the way. I had to stay with her. I tried to get her off the drugs but she would slip out when I was asleep. Then she came home stoned, or not at all. I was at my wit's end. Then one night she had clearly taken a large dose of something. She was completely out of it. I told her we were going for a drive and she just got into the car like a lamb. I brought her back here.'

Dolly seemed to go into a trance. Tom leaned over and touched her hand. 'Dolly? What happened?'

'I took care of her like a baby. I got Mossie to get me Methadone. Apart from that I warned him to stay away from her, and he did. After a few weeks, when she was calmer, I went to visit Una. I didn't take any chances. I made sure that Mossie was going to be out that day too,' she assured Tom and then stared off into the distance. 'I wasn't gone for more than a few hours but when I came back she wasn't in her room. There was a letter on her bed. I knew, without even opening it, what she had done. I found her in the garage, hanging from the beam. I tried to get her down and save her but it was too late.'

'That is awful, I'm sorry.' Tom gripped her hand between his.

Dolly stared down at her tears, dropping on to their joined hands. After a while, Tom went in search of drinks and poured her a glass of gin.

'What was in the letter?' he asked after she had swallowed some.

'Everything,' she said, her voice so quiet he had to lean closer to hear. 'How nice he'd been to her at first. How, on their days out, he'd buy chocolate for her and a little bottle of vodka for himself. If she was good, he'd give her a tiny drop. How, when he'd go to her room to say goodnight, he'd give her something to make her pain go away. Something to help her sleep, to stop the nightmares, to dry her tears. He was very crafty. He didn't rush it,' Dolly said, her eyes full of hate. 'This went on for weeks. And then one day he said he was too busy to take her out and when he went in to say goodnight, he brought no magic pill. She cried and begged him for something. Of course, he had given in then. Told her he would do anything to make her happy, would she do anything for him?'

'And she was ready to do whatever it took to get high,' Tom said, shaking his head. He saw this kind of thing all the time in his job.

'Anything and everything,' Dolly said and she searched his face with desperate eyes. 'How could I not see what was going on? What kind of bloody fool was I?'

'There is no point beating yourself up, Dolly—'

'Do you know what?' Dolly said, almost as if she had not heard him. 'Linda felt guilty. She said sorry to me! He had abused her, stolen her innocence and turned her into an addict, and in her letter, she asked for forgiveness, when it was all my fault.'

'No, Dolly, it was his fault. I'm surprised you didn't kill him.' Tom tried not to feel a heel. He was leading her on to get a result.

She raised her eyes to meet his. 'That was Plan A.'

Chapter Nine

Dolly opened her mouth to continue but he held up his hand to stop her. If she admitted to anything he would have to act on it. Now, to his surprise, he really didn't want to. This woman had suffered enough, was still suffering. He didn't want her to confess to something and force him to take her in. 'Maybe you should talk to your lawyer before you say anything else, Dolly.'

She stared at him and started to laugh. 'I can't believe a guard is telling me not to talk! It's very nice of you,

Detective, but don't worry about me. Right now the only confession I'm making is to being stupid and blind and letting Mossie play me for a fool.'

'He fooled us all,' he told her. 'Let's drop the detective, Dolly. I'm not here on business. We're just two friends having a chat.'

'Us? Friends?' she jeered, raising her eyebrows.

He grinned. 'Ah, sure, why not?'

She stood up and went to the cabinet to fetch another glass. 'Friends it is. For tonight at least.'

He held up a hand as she started to pour. 'I'm driving.'

'Trust me, *friend*, it will be well out of your system by the time I've finished telling this story.'

He watched as she poured them two large measures. He took a drink as she lit another cigarette. 'So, Plan A was abandoned.'

'Plan A was too good for him. Anyway, the night that Linda died, I wasn't able for anything. But I didn't trust myself around him. I knew he'd sense that I was on to him and then I would be in danger. I had to go somewhere he couldn't find me, somewhere that I could figure out what to do next. So I went to The Mill House.' Dolly took a sip of her drink.

'The spa?' Tom sat up. 'The hotel in that flier you showed me?'

Dolly nodded. 'Yes, but it's not a hotel. It's a safe house of sorts for women like me, married to criminals and living in danger or fear.'

Tom thought of the glossy flier and shook his head. 'But what about the real guests?'

She gave him a grim smile. 'There aren't any. You only get to visit The Mill House if you are invited. Any outsiders who call looking for a room are told it's fully booked.' She gave a dry laugh. 'So it has a name for being posh and select. Which is gas as it's not like that at all. But it is peaceful. Somewhere to escape when we need to. The men see the flier and swallow it all and any woman who goes there promises not to talk about it. And, trust me, they don't, because they want to be able to go back. We are only allowed to tell another woman who is in the same situation and even then, she doesn't know the full story until she gets there.' Dolly looked up at him and glared. 'You better keep your mouth shut about this.'

'Of course I will,' he assured her. 'Who pays for it all?'

'Mags Breslin set it up. Ever hear of her?' Dolly cocked an eyebrow at him.

He frowned and shook his head. He was learning a hell of a lot today.

'Pat Breslin was probably before your time. He had brothels all over the country. Very successful he was too. But he used to knock the crap out of Mags. She lost two babies as a result. When Pat died of a stroke, Mags set up The Mill House. Women who can afford it are asked to leave a donation, but anyone who is skint is just as welcome. A good woman, Mags.' Dolly drew deep on her fag.

'She sounds it. I can't believe that no one knows about it. Does anyone live there?' Tom was amazed that they had kept this place a secret.

'Yes, some of the staff are ex-wives of cons. I'm sure there's a long list of women who would kill to work there.' She grinned. 'Pardon the pun.'

'And that's how you met Ro—' He stopped, cursing himself. He wasn't going to put words in Dolly's mouth. Certainly not about Rose.

Dolly smiled. 'You're smarter than I gave you credit for, Detective. I met . . .

a woman there a couple of months ago. She had just found out her brother was dead and she had an idea that he might have been murdered by someone she knew.'

'So what did she do?' he asked, not sure he wanted to hear the answer.

'Do?' Dolly looked at him as if he was mad. 'Nothing, of course. You don't have a wife or children, do you, Detective?'

He paused for a moment, overcome with sadness, and then shook his head. 'No.'

'Even if she could have got away from her husband, she knew there was no chance she would be allowed to take the child with her. So she did the only thing she could do. She went to The Mill House for a few days so that she could mourn in private before going back and putting on a brave face for the sake of her son.'

'I see,' he said slowly. 'So how did you get talking?'

'I arrived, had a massage – yes, there are treatments and classes but they are all about helping us to relax. Then I went down to the bar for a drink,' Dolly continued. 'This woman was alone at the end of the bar. Milling into the drink, she was. She went to get up to go to the ladies and I saw her sway. I caught her just before she hit the deck. I helped her to the bathroom and then found us a quiet corner and ordered a pot of coffee.'

'That was good of you.'

'We look after each other at The Mill House. To be honest, I was glad to listen to someone else's problems. I didn't want to think about my own.' Dolly's eyes darkened with sadness.

Tom found himself leaning forward in his seat. 'And?'

Dolly gave him a knowing smile and reached for her cigarettes. 'You've fallen under her spell too.'

This bloody woman is far too sharp, Tom thought. 'I'm just trying to get some answers. I'd like to help you both, make sure that you never have to fear anyone again.' He kept his tone neutral.

'Ha! Who do you think you are, God? Anyway, she told me all about her brother, her little boy and that bastard of a husband.' Dolly's eyes twinkled. 'May he rest in peace.'

'Why was he a bastard . . . in particular?' Tom wanted the lowdown.

'Her brother was an addict and owed a fortune to her husband's family. So they did what's usually done. They made him work for them.'

'Dealing?'

Dolly nodded. 'When she found out, she was shocked. This woman had grown up in a very different world. The brother was her only family. Top of his class in university. I think he was going to be an accountant or broker or something in that line.'

'Was she working?' he asked.

'She was. A teacher before she got married. Anyway, she couldn't get her brother off the drugs and as long as he was using, he had to work for O'Dowd. She got this bright idea of contacting his "boss" to try to persuade him to agree to a payment plan.'

Tom groaned. He could see where this was going. 'But the boss had a better idea?'

'You got it. She was lucky in a way. He could have just used her and tossed her aside, but he fell for her.' Dolly gave him a shrewd look. 'You can understand that.'

Tom ignored the remark.

'He said if she married him, not only would he write off the lad's debt, but he would pay for him go into a treatment centre and start a new life abroad.'

'And she believed him?' Tom said in dismay. How could Rose have thought that someone like O'Dowd would keep his word?

'Yes, and she planned to do a moonlight flit once the brother was safe.'

Tom silently cursed Rose's innocence.

'Of course, he was wise to her,' Dolly said. 'He knew she was way out of his league. He knew that she didn't give a damn about him, so he made sure she never went anywhere without a minder. You can imagine, once he knew that there was a baby on the way, she was more or less under house arrest. And she'd done it all for nothing. Her brother was dead.'

'And that's when you came up with Plan B.' Tom said, his heart sinking.

Had Rose and Dolly joined forces to rid themselves of their husbands?

Dolly clinked her glass against his, smiling. 'I have no idea what you mean, Detective. Now, if you or any other filth want to talk to me in future, give me some notice so I can bring along my lawyer.'

He nodded. 'Of course. You know, Dolly, you have Linda's letter. If it's as damning as you say, Mossie would go down for a good few years, I'm sure of it.'

She looked up at him, her eyes cold and hard. 'That's Plan C.'

Chapter Ten

Tom made his way to the park armed
with a newspaper and a large coffee.
Shay had tipped him off that Rose was
back in the country but now living on
the south side of the city. He could not
help himself. He had to see her. It was
the third time he had come and sat on
this bench among the trees opposite the
playground. He had smiled as he
watched Rose push Toby on the swing.
The child would scream in delight as he
went higher and higher. How the boy
had grown in the eight months since he

had first met mother and child. Tom was glad to see that Toby looked nothing like his dad. He was sure that Rose was happy about that too.

Tom had not seen Dolly since the day of their chat. She had gone to the station in Limerick and admitted to framing Mossie because he had abused her niece. Plan C was underway. She had refused police protection while she waited for her case to come to trial. She was in the custody of her cousin but they had moved, Tom suspected they were at The Mill House. He hoped she wasn't 'helping' any other women with their marital problems. Tom knew from the talk in the station that Dolly hadn't mentioned Rose. She had said that in her grief, she just wanted to set Mossie up and hadn't given much thought to which bastard to take out. It had to be someone at the top of the drugs scene. It was bad luck for Gerry that he had been in the news that week. His name had been linked to some bad drugs on Dublin streets that had resulted in the death of a few teenagers. Tom didn't believe her reason but it was a good one. He was grateful that he hadn't had to take the woman in. Grateful for her quick thinking, that she had left Rose out of it. And he had to admire her strength and loyalty. There was some sense of crazy justice in what she had done. She probably felt honour-bound to do it on behalf of her sister and niece and the sisterhood of criminals' wives. A good barrister would probably get her a short sentence for Gerry's murder. Perhaps plead temporary insanity due to Dolly discovering her niece's body and the suicide note.

As if enough wasn't going on, the Guards got an anonymous call with information about Ronan, Rose's brother. It was directions to a quiet spot in the Dublin Mountains where they might find a body. A few days later, the remains were discovered. Tom had longed to be the one to break the news to poor Rose but it was best if he kept his distance. He was working on several other cases so he left it to Shay Scanlan. Anyway, he was still afraid that if he looked into Rose O'Dowd's beautiful eyes he might see guilt there, that she and Dolly were in this together.

Rose and Toby now lived in an apartment in Sandymount. A nice and secure complex. Tom didn't think she would be here for long though. She and Toby would most likely disappear once the O'Dowds relaxed their hold on her. Scanlan didn't think that would happen anytime soon.

'Why do you say that?' Tom had asked.

'Jude was there the last day we dropped by and it was clear that she is terrified of him.'

'Do you think he's hurting her?' Tom had struggled to sound cool. All he could think of was how Gerry had blackmailed her into his bed. The thought that she might have been passed on to the creep's little brother made him feel sick with rage.

'No, I don't think so. Our Jude isn't into women. He just wants her where he can keep an eye on her and make sure that Toby grows up as an O'Dowd.'

That thought sickened Tom as, he imagined it sickened Rose. When she said that her life was just beginning, had she forgotten that she would still be a part of the O'Dowd family? That they would not let her or Toby go easily. But why the hell did he care? She wasn't his problem and yet . . . a part of him wished that she was.

'Detective Inspector Doyle?'

He almost jumped out of his skin when he looked up and saw Rose standing over him. He had been so lost in thought, he had not noticed her arrive. He stared at her, lost for words.

She looked embarrassed. 'You don't remember me. Rose O'Dowd. Well, Rose Fitzgerald now, again.'

'Of course I remember.' He stood up. 'How are you?'

'We're fine.' She looked over to where Toby was trying in vain to scramble up the slide. 'No, Toby, stop that!' She sped off to rescue him. Tom followed more slowly, smiling as she swept her son up in her arms and kissed him.

He took a moment to study her. She looked bloody great. Her skinny jeans and pink top showed off her lovely figure. Her glossy hair hung in a long braid over one shoulder. She threw back her head and laughed, a joyous sound, showing off even white teeth. As she set the child down, he caught sight of Tom and waved.

Tom joined them. 'Hello, Toby.'

'Hi,' he said before charging off to join another toddler on the roundabout.

Rose looked up at him, curious. 'Do you live around here?'

'No, I have an appointment,' he nodded towards the main street in the distance, 'and I'm far too early. I heard you'd moved. Is it nice around here?'

'It is when I'm left to enjoy it in peace.' She pulled a face.

'Your in-laws?' he asked.

'Yes,' she said, her voice hard.

'Sorry to hear about your brother.'

'Thank you. I suspected he was dead but it was good that I could lay him to rest. No thanks to the O'Dowds,' she added bitterly.

'Do you think they were responsible for Ronan's death?'

'Gerry was. I'm sure of it,' Rose declared.

'His brothers may have been involved and could be charged,' Tom told her.

'The Guards won't get anything on Robbie and Jude. Trust me, that family knows how to cover their tracks.'

'Yet someone came forward and told us where your brother's remains were,' he pointed out.

'That was because you lot offered a reward,' she reminded him, going to help Toby onto the swing.

Tom followed her and stood watching as she settled Toby in the harness and started to push him. 'We didn't offer any reward, Rose. It was someone else.'

'Who?' she asked, surprised.

He looked at her. 'Off the record? I believe it came from Mossie Maher's bank account, with a little help from Dolly.'

She looked even more confused. 'Dolly?'

'Yes, you remember Dolly. You met at The Mill House?' He watched her carefully.

Rose blushed. 'I remember. She was *very* kind to me.'

'Life is mad, isn't it? The day that Gerry died and her husband was accused of his murder, Dolly buried her only niece.'

Rose slumped onto the bench and stared up at him, shocked. 'Dolly is that man's wife? No, you must be mistaken. It can't be the same woman.'

'It is.' A wave of relief rolled over him. This was no act. Rose really had no idea that the woman she'd poured her heart out to was Mossie's wife. Which meant that she had had no part in Plan B. She was *innocent*.

'But I don't understand. This makes no sense. Why on earth would she put up a reward to help find my brother?'

He hesitated. He shouldn't be talking to Rose. He shouldn't even be here. He was already treading a thin line. 'You have more in common than you realise. Look, I'm not on this case anymore. I've said too much already. Someone will be in touch very soon to let you know the latest developments. I should get going.'

'Hang on a second,' she said, her eyes blazing. 'You think I had something to do with Gerry's death, don't you?'

'I had my suspicions,' he admitted. 'That's my job. But not anymore. And even if you had, Rose, I wouldn't have blamed you,' he added gently.

'Thanks a lot!' she said, her eyes hurt. 'I didn't kill Gerry, Tom.'

'I know that . . . now. Like I said, it's my job to look at everyone as a possible suspect.' But he could see she was still upset. That she didn't understand why he thought she might be involved in her husband's murder. 'Okay, look, Dolly Maher has confessed to framing her husband.'

Rose gasped. 'Dolly? But why?'

'It seems Mossie was abusing his niece. So, although he's been cleared of your husband's murder, he is still behind bars. I imagine he will be for a long time. The evidence is strong. '

'Oh, God, Linda! That was her name, wasn't it? Dolly told me. The bastard. He deserves all he gets.' She crossed her arms around her and shivered.

'I agree.' He took a card from his jacket pocket and handed it to Rose. 'Look, err, if, well, you ever need to talk to someone...' His words were so clumsy, he felt like a bloody schoolboy. He studied his feet. 'About, well, anything.' He risked looking at her. 'You are always welcome to call me.'

She nodded. 'Thanks.'

'Well, see you round.' He turned to walk away.

'Tom?'

He stopped and looked back at her. 'Yes, Rose?'

'You knew I'd be here this morning, didn't you?' she said, searching his eyes.

He gave her a sheepish grin. 'Guilty. I just wanted to, no, needed to make sure that you were both okay.'

Her eyes widened. 'You came here just to see me?'

'Yes,' he admitted.

She bent her head and studied his card. 'I *could* do with talking to someone . . . now and again.' She looked up at him with a shy smile.

'Really?' Tom said, his heart lifting. 'We could go for a coffee now, if you want. Unless you are in a hurry.'

She raised her eyebrows. 'But what about your appointment, Tom?'

He grinned. 'What appointment?'

She laughed. 'There is a nice place just around the corner. Toby loves their muffins.'

'That sounds good to me, Rose.'

She smiled happily and held his gaze for a moment longer. 'Okay then.'

'Okay then,' he said, now grinning like an idiot. He watched as she went to get Toby and heard him cheer when she told him the plan. They came back to join him, hand in hand.

'Muffin! Yum!' The child beamed up at him.

Tom patted Toby's head and looked at Rose's beautiful, smiling face.

'Yum, indeed,' he agreed.